Look Out, Jeremy Bean!

BY **ALICE SCHERTLE**

ILLUSTRATED BY **DAVID SLONIM**

chronicle books · san francisco

Contents

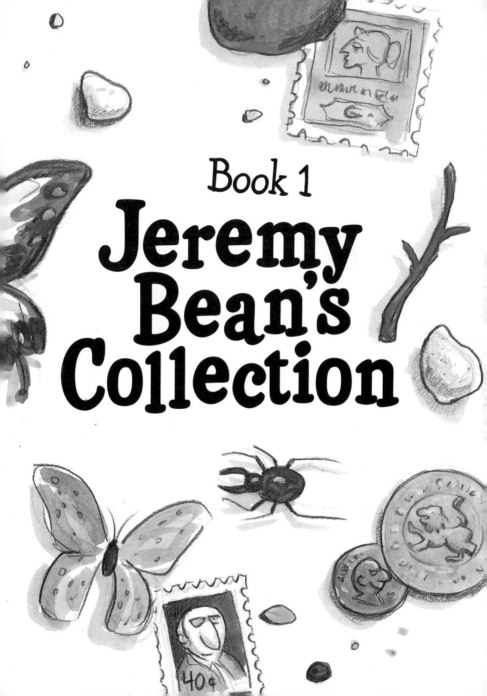

Book 1

Jeremy Bean's Collection

Seeds and Cookies

One day Jeremy Bean's friend Max brought his seed collection to school. There were hairy seeds and wrinkled seeds and seeds as smooth as marbles. There were flower seeds and seeds from trees. Everyone gathered around to see.

"Tomorrow," said Ms. Tucker, "anyone else who has a collection may bring it to school to share."

"After school I'm going to work on my collection," said Winnie.

"Me too," said Luke.

"Me too," said Jeremy Bean.

Jeremy hurried into the kitchen. He almost ran into his grandfather, who was making cookies.

"Whoa!" said Gramps. "What's the rush?"

"I have to start a collection," Jeremy told him. "I have to start one *right away*!"

"Too bad," said Gramps. "I was hoping you would have time to lick the bowl."

"I think I have time for that," said Jeremy Bean.

"Grammsh," said Jeremy with a mouth full of cookie dough, "did you ever have a collection?"

"When I was a boy," said Gramps, "I collected eggs from the chickens. But my collections only lasted until breakfast." Gramps laughed.

"Tell about Ralph the Gentleman Rooster," said Jeremy. It was his favorite story.

"Well now," Gramps began, "most roosters are mean and bossy. But not Ralph. Ralph was a gentleman. When I fed the chickens, Ralph always let the hens eat first. When Ralph scratched up some bugs, he let the hens snatch up the big ones. Those hens knew they could push him around."

"So you brought him inside," said Jeremy.

Gramps nodded. "I snuck him into the house. Ralph and I had cherry pie in the kitchen, where the grabby hens couldn't get it."

Jeremy giggled. "Tell about the floor."

"Oh, yes," said Gramps. "Ralph always pooped on the floor. I had to follow him around with a mop. Ralph was a gentleman, but he was also a rooster."

Jeremy put his empty bowl in the sink. "If we had chickens," he said, "I'd collect the eggs. But I'm going to make a special collection. Something no one else will have."

"When you're through," said Gramps, "come down and collect some cookies."

Sticks and Stones

Jeremy ran upstairs to his room. He got his old sneakers out of the closet. He put them in a big shopping bag. He put his sandals in the bag. He found one lone rain boot and dropped it into the bag. Then he took off the shoes he was wearing and dropped them in too.

Next Jeremy collected shoes from his mother's closet. He collected his father's bedroom slippers. He went into Gramps's room and collected more shoes.

"What are you doing, Jeremy?" asked Mom.

"I'm making a collection," Jeremy told her. "Would you mind taking off your shoes?"

"Jeremy," said Mom, "these belong to other people. You can't collect other people's shoes."

"How about hats?" said Jeremy.

"Nope," said Mom. "But I know you can find something else to collect. Right after you put the shoes away."

Jeremy put all the shoes back in the proper closets. Then he went outside. He picked up a rock with little shiny specks on it.

"Rocks don't belong to anybody," said Jeremy Bean. "A rock collection might be nice." He put the rock in his pocket.

He found a stick shaped like a snake.

"Sticks don't belong to anybody," said

Jeremy. "A stick collection might be nice."

A green bug ran down the stick.

"A bug collection might be nice too," said Jeremy Bean. He put the stick and the bug in his pocket.

Jeremy decided to see how Winnie and Luke were doing.

Winnie was in her backyard. She had a pail of water and a scrub brush. She showed Jeremy her rock collection.

"Aren't they pretty?" said Winnie. "When I scrub the dirt off, you can see the colors."

Jeremy took the shiny rock out of his pocket.

"Oh, no," said Winnie. "Are you doing rocks too?"

"No," said Jeremy. "I'm doing something different. This is for you."

Luke was in his garage. He had a piece of sandpaper in his hand.

"Look at my stick collection," he said to Jeremy. "I sand the wood nice and smooth."

Jeremy took the snake stick out of his pocket.

"Uh-oh," said Luke. "Are you doing sticks too?"

"No," said Jeremy. "I'm doing something different. This is for you."

On the way home, Jeremy thought about stamps and coins.

"*Everybody* does stamps and coins!" he thought. "Everybody does *everything*! How can I go to school tomorrow without a collection of my own?"

Jeremy remembered the bug. He felt in his pocket. He turned the pocket inside out.

"I guess he didn't want to be collected," said Jeremy Bean. "I'm going to be the only kid in the whole class with no collection at all."

A Story

Gramps was taking cookies out of the oven.

"How's the collection coming along?" he asked.

"No good," said Jeremy. "Mom won't let me collect shoes. Everything else is taken."

Jeremy slumped down in a chair. "I'm the only kid in the whole world without a collection."

Gramps nodded. "The world is full of collectors."

"Even my bug didn't want to be collected," said Jeremy.

"I don't blame him," said Gramps. He piled warm cookies on a plate.

"I'll never think of something different," said Jeremy. "I'll never have a collection of my own."

"When I was a boy," said Gramps, "eating cookies always helped me think."

"Me too," said Jeremy. He helped himself to three big cookies. "Will you tell me a story while I eat them?"

"Let me think," said Gramps and popped a cookie into his mouth.

"Well now, when I was a boy, I built a tree house. I built it high in the branches of an oak tree. I kept two old pillows in it and a box of cookies."

Gramps closed his eyes and smiled.

"I lay back on those pillows and munched cookies and thought about things. I did my best thinking in that tree house. I think it was the cookies that did it."

Jeremy helped himself to two more. "Just think," he said. "You were a little kid like me."

"Yes," said Gramps. "And just think. Some day you will be a big kid like me."

Suddenly Jeremy jumped to his feet.

"Thanks, Gramps!" said Jeremy. "Thanks for the cookies and for the story and for the idea."

"The idea?" asked Gramps.

"Yes," said Jeremy. "You have given me a *great* idea for my collection!"

Jeremy's Collection

The next morning Jeremy met Winnie and Luke on the way to school.

Winnie had her rock collection in a bag.

Luke had his stick collection in a box.

"Where's your collection?" they asked together.

Jeremy smiled a mysterious smile. "I have it with me," he said.

"Is it in your pocket?" asked Luke.

"I can't put it in my pocket," said Jeremy.

"Is it in your lunch box?" asked Winnie.

"I can't put it in my lunch box," said Jeremy.

Luke said, "What is it?"

"You'll see," said Jeremy Bean.

At school, Winnie and Luke laid out their collections on the science table.

"Aren't you going to set up your collection?" Luke asked Jeremy.

"I can't put my collection on the table," Jeremy said.

"You can't put it in your pocket," said Winnie. "You can't put it in your lunch box. You can't even put it on the table. What is it?"

Jeremy smiled a mysterious smile. "You'll see," he said.

That morning the class shared their collections.

When it was Jeremy's turn, he walked to the front of the room.

"I am going to tell you a story," he said.

"It's about me. I tried to collect shoes, but Mom made me put them back. I collected a rock, but Winnie was already doing rocks. I collected a stick, but Luke was already doing sticks. The bug I collected ran away.

"My gramps gave me some cookies to help me think. He told me a story about a tree house he built. Sometimes he tells me about Ralph the Gentleman Rooster. My Gramps has lots of stories about when he was a little kid.

"So I decided to collect stories about me. I will tell them to my grandchildren when I'm as old as Gramps. And this is the first story in my collection," said Jeremy Bean.

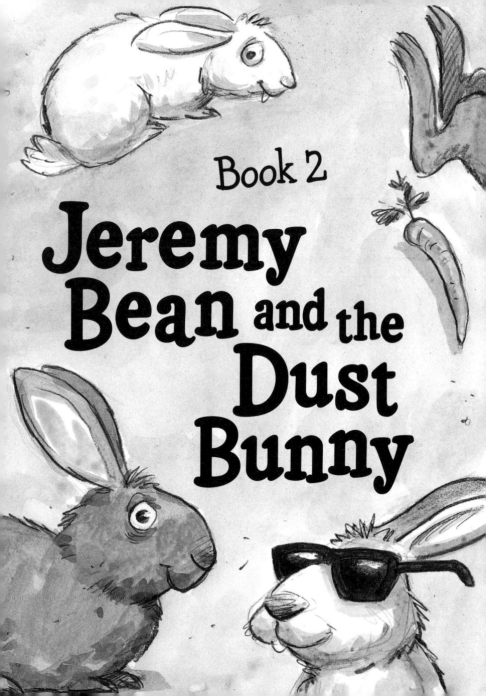

Book 2

Jeremy Bean and the Dust Bunny

Dust Bunnies!

Jeremy Bean's mom was talking on the telephone. Jeremy was listening.

"I will be busy tomorrow," said Jeremy's mom. "There are dust bunnies under the beds. I have to get after them."

"Dust bunnies!" thought Jeremy Bean. "Under the beds!"

Jeremy had never seen a dust bunny. But he was sure that a dust bunny would make a wonderful pet. He knew he would have to work fast. Last year Mom got after the mice in the attic. Pretty soon there wasn't a mouse left.

Jeremy hurried out to the garage. He pulled a stack of cardboard boxes off a dusty shelf. He lifted out all the smaller boxes and chose the bottom one.

"Better make it big," said Jeremy. "A dust bunny needs plenty of room."

Jeremy put some leaves in the box. He put some grass in too.

"A dust bunny likes a soft bed," said Jeremy.

He put a water dish in the box.

"Dust bunnies get thirsty," said Jeremy Bean.

Jeremy carried the box into his bedroom and put it on the floor. He filled the dish with water and put it back in the box. Then he sat down to wait.

The Bunny Trap

Jeremy waited a long time. Then he tiptoed to his bed and looked under it.

Jeremy saw his model airplane, a felt-tip pen, a sock, and his missing rain boot. He did not see any dust bunnies.

"Here, bunny, bunny, bunny," he called.

Jeremy got a flashlight and crawled under the bed. He shined the light into all the corners. He shined it into the rain boot.

"ATCHOO!" Jeremy sneezed. "Now I have scared them. Dust bunnies are afraid of loud noises."

Jeremy went into the kitchen. He got a carrot, a piece of cheese, a slice of cold pizza, an apple, a cupcake, a graham cracker, and a granola bar. Jeremy put everything in a bag and carried it to his room.

He made a long line of food from the bed to the box. Then he sat down and waited. He waited . . . and waited. . . .

"Dust bunnies are shy," thought Jeremy. "They will never come out while I'm here."

Jeremy stood up. In a loud voice he said, "I GUESS I WILL GO AWAY NOW. I WILL GO INTO MY CLOSET AND LOOK AT MY CLOTHES. I WILL NOT COME OUT FOR A LONG TIME."

Jeremy went into his closet and closed the door. After a while he opened the door a crack. *Creak!* went the door.

"This will never work," thought Jeremy Bean. "The dust bunnies know I'm here. They are still afraid."

Jeremy came out of the closet. He was carrying a suitcase.

"TIME FOR MY TRIP TO MEXICO," he said loudly.

He picked up the pizza and took a bite.

"DELICIOUS!" said Jeremy Bean. "THIS IS THE BEST FOOD I EVER TASTED. I WILL EAT IT ALL UP WHEN I GET BACK FROM MEXICO . . . UNLESS SOMEONE EATS IT UP WHILE I AM GONE."

Jeremy walked out with the suitcase.

In a little while he was sneaking back toward his room. He was wrapped in a blanket. He had a lampshade on his head. Jeremy stood in the doorway and acted like a lamp.

"What have we here?" said Dad. He leaned over to take a better look. "I don't remember this lamp. Must be a new one. I wonder where you turn it on."

Dad began to poke the blanket with his finger. He was poking Jeremy in the ribs.

Jeremy laughed. "That tickles!" he said.

"A talking lamp!" said Dad. "What a good idea!"

"It's your son," said Jeremy. "I'm not really a lamp."

"Nonsense," said Dad. "I've known my son for years. He doesn't look like this."

Jeremy took off the blanket.

"It *is* Jeremy!" cried Dad. "I am glad I found you. Dinner is ready. Please don't wear your shade to the table."

Monster Bunny

After dinner, Jeremy took a big bowl up to his room. He yawned and lay down on his bed.

"I'M GOING TO SLEEP NOW," said Jeremy Bean loudly. "I WILL NOT WAKE UP UNTIL MORNING."

Jeremy held the bowl over the edge of his bed. He was ready to pop it over the head of the first dust bunny he saw.

In the middle of the night, Jeremy Bean sat up. Something under his bed was going *bump! bump!* At the foot of his bed he saw two long fuzzy things. *Bump! Bump!* He saw big pink eyes, long white whiskers, and teeth. A huge bunny looked down at Jeremy. When it moved, puffs of dust floated up in the air.

"Dinner's ready," said the bunny in a deep voice.

"Dinner?" said Jeremy. "I'm not hungry."

"I am," said the bunny.

Jeremy looked at the long yellow teeth.

"Would you like a carrot?" he asked.

"Dust bunnies don't eat carrots," said the deep voice.

"How about a granola bar?" asked Jeremy.

The dust bunny shook his head. Puffs of dust flew around. It moved a little closer.

"Graham cracker?" said Jeremy quickly. "Pizza? Apple? Cupcake? Cheese?"

The big pink eyes stared at Jeremy Bean.

"That's not what dust bunnies eat," said the deep voice.

Jeremy scooted back against the pillow.

"What *do* dust bunnies eat?" he asked in a small voice.

"Dust bunnies eat BEANS!" boomed the bunny.

"Beans?" squeaked Jeremy. "You mean lima beans? String beans? Refried beans?"

The big head leaned closer and closer.

"I mean JEREMY BEANS!"

Jeremy pulled the blanket over his head.

"NO!" he shouted. "Go away! Go away! Go away!"

Two hands grabbed Jeremy.

Saved!

"Wake up," said Mom. "Wake up, Jeremy."

Jeremy looked around. Mom was holding him tight. No one else was in the room.

"There was a dust bunny!" said Jeremy. "He tried to *get* me!"

"A what?" said Mom. "A dust bunny?"

"Yes," said Jeremy. "I heard you talking about dust bunnies. I tried to catch one. But tonight one almost caught *me*!"

"Jeremy," said Mom, "let me show you a dust bunny."

Mom reached under the bed. She held up a small gray ball of dust.

"People call these dust bunnies," she said.

Dad poked his head in the doorway.

"What's going on?" he asked. "A party?"

Jeremy told Dad about the dust bunnies. He showed Dad the box and the water dish.

"It's a good bunny box," said Dad. "I wonder if it would do for a hamster."

"Oh, yes," said Jeremy. "It would be fine for a hamster."

"Tomorrow," said Dad, "we will go to the pet shop."

"Yes," said Mom. "And tomorrow, we will all catch dust bunnies."

"With the vacuum," said Jeremy Bean.

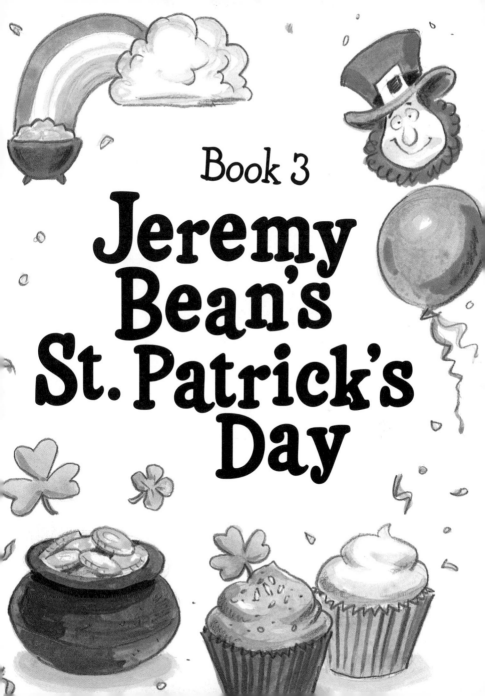

Book 3

Jeremy Bean's St. Patrick's Day

Party Plans

Jeremy Bean was on his way to school. He hummed a tune. This would be a good day. It was the day before Saint Patrick's Day. His class was going to plan a party.

Jeremy ran across the playground, up the big stone steps, and into the hall. There was Mr. Dudley, the principal of the whole school. Jeremy would have to walk past him.

Jeremy Bean slowed down. He stopped humming. Maybe today was not such a good day after all.

Jeremy wasn't exactly *afraid* of Mr. Dudley. Not exactly *afraid*. It was just that

the principal was so tall and so bald and had such a big brown mustache and such a big, deep voice. He made Jeremy feel very small and very shy.

"HI THERE," said Mr. Dudley in his big, deep voice.

Jeremy looked down at his shoes.

"Hi," he said in a small voice.

"Happy Day Before Saint Patrick's Day," said Mr. Dudley.

Jeremy didn't know what to say. So he didn't say anything. He just hurried down the hall and into his room.

That morning Ms. Tucker read a story about Saint Patrick. Then everyone drew pictures of him.

Jeremy gave him long hair and a long gray beard but no mustache.

"Who knows the Saint Patrick's Day color?" asked Ms. Tucker.

"Green!" shouted everyone at once.

"Let's think of some green food," said Ms. Tucker. "We'll have green food for our party."

Jeremy's class decided to have celery, green apples, pickles, lime punch, and cupcakes with green frosting.

"Wear something green tomorrow," said Lulu. "Everyone in the whole school will be wearing green."

"I'll wear my Alligator Man T-shirt," said Luke.

"I'll ask if I can wear my mama's green necklace," said Winnie.

"I have green socks," said Max. "I'll wear those."

"I'll wear my green sweater," said Jeremy Bean.

Jeremy hurried home after school. He took his green sweater out of the closet.

"This will be perfect," he said. "I better not forget it."

He tied the sweater around his waist. Then he kicked the soccer ball around the backyard.

At dinner he rolled the sweater up and sat on it.

"Jeremy is getting taller," said Mom.

After dinner, Jeremy tied the sweater around his neck. He played superhero until bedtime. Then he put the sweater on over his pajamas.

In the middle of the night, Jeremy woke up. He was too hot. So he took off the green sweater.

Green and Mean

The next morning Jeremy got dressed. He made his bed. Jeremy's bed was always lumpy after he made it. Today one lump was very big, but Jeremy didn't notice.

On the way to school he saw Mr. Lee working on his car. Jeremy smiled and waved.

"Happy Saint Patrick's Day!" called Mr. Lee.

Jeremy stopped walking. He stopped smiling. He looked down at his clothes.

Yellow shirt, blue pants . . . *no green*!

Jeremy pulled up his pant legs. Brown shoes, white socks . . . *no green*!

He checked his underwear even though he knew he didn't have green underwear.

Just then Winnie and Luke walked up.

"Uh-oh," said Luke. "Jeremy's not wearing green."

He and Winnie skipped off, singing,

> *"Jeremy Bean*
> *didn't wear green!*
> *Jeremy Bean*
> *didn't wear green!"*

Jeremy picked some leaves. He stuck them into his shirt pocket. Then he hurried off to school.

In the school yard, Lulu said, "Where's your green, Jeremy?"

Jeremy showed her the leaves.

"Leaves don't count," said Max.

"Jeremy Bean didn't wear green!" sang Lulu.

Pretty soon everyone was singing,

> *"Jeremy Bean*
> *didn't wear green!*
> *Jeremy Bean*
> *didn't wear green!"*

"STOP IT!" shouted Jeremy. He ran into the school.

There was Mr. Dudley, standing in the hall. He was wearing a green hat, a green jacket, and a green bow tie. He was looking down at some papers in his hand.

Jeremy didn't wait for Mr. Dudley to look up. He darted into a closet and closed the door.

The closet smelled like soap and paint and floor wax. Jeremy squeezed in between a ladder and a push broom. He stood there in the dark and wondered: What would Mr. Dudley say to someone who forgot to wear green on Saint Patrick's Day?

Jeremy heard footsteps.

The closet door opened slowly.

Mr. Dudley, the principal of the whole school, looked down at Jeremy.

"Will you please come to my office?" he said.

An Invitation

·Principal's Office·

Jeremy had never been in the principal's office before. He stood in front of the big desk and waited.

He waited for Mr. Dudley to say, "Where is your green, Jeremy Bean?"

He waited for Mr. Dudley to say, "Don't you know the rules?"

"You know, Jeremy," said Mr. Dudley, "I have too much work to do. Sometimes I feel like hiding in the broom closet."

"You do?" said Jeremy.

"Oh yes," said the principal. "I'd like to

hide from these papers. Look at all these papers on my desk. Do you think you could help me?"

Jeremy helped Mr. Dudley stack the papers in neat piles. He stapled some of them together. He put paper clips on others.

"I'm pretty good at papers," said Jeremy.

"You're a good helper," said Mr. Dudley.

He didn't ask why Jeremy wasn't wearing green. He didn't even ask why Jeremy had been in the broom closet.

They talked about soccer and doughnuts and their favorite TV shows.

After a while, Jeremy said, "I forgot my green sweater today. Everybody was teasing me."

"Well," said Mr. Dudley, "as you can see, I'm wearing plenty of green. I think I can spare some."

He put his hat on Jeremy's head. But it wasn't quite right.

He let Jeremy try on his jacket. But that wasn't quite right either.

Then Mr. Dudley tied his green bow tie around Jeremy's neck. And it was perfect.

Jeremy looked up at the very big smile under Mr. Dudley's very big mustache.

"Mr. Dudley," he said, "would you like to come to our Saint Patrick's Day party?"

"I'd be delighted," said Mr. Dudley in his nice deep voice.

Jeremy and the principal of the whole school walked to class together.

"My friend Jeremy Bean invited me to the party," said Mr. Dudley.

"My friend Mr. Dudley lent me his bow tie," said Jeremy Bean.

They sat down and helped themselves to celery, green apples, pickles, lime punch, and cupcakes with green frosting.

Jeremy and Winnie and Luke walked home from school together.

"Wow!" said Luke. "Mr. Dudley let you keep his bow tie!"

"Lucky you!" said Winnie. "I wish *I* forgot to wear green."

Jeremy smiled. He felt the tie under his chin. "Mr. Dudley's a nice guy," he said. "Sometimes he feels like hiding in the broom closet like I did."

"Wow!" said Winnie. "You hid in the broom closet?"

"Yep," said Jeremy. "That was just the beginning. This whole day goes into my story collection."

"Tell it," said Luke.

"Tell the whole thing," said Winnie.

And Jeremy did.

First paperback edition published in 2011 by Chronicle Books LLC.

Text ©1987, 2009 by Alice Schertle.
Illustrations ©2009 by David Slonim.
Jeremy Bean's St. Patrick's Day was first published in 1987.
First Chronicle Books edition published in 2009.

The Library of Congress has cataloged the original edition as follows:
Schertle, Alice.
Look out, Jeremy Bean! / by Alice Schertle ; illustrated by David Slonim.
p. cm.
Contains the previously published book Jeremy Bean's St. Patrick's Day.
Contents: Jeremy Bean's collection — Jeremy Bean and the dust bunny —
Jeremy Bean's St. Patrick's Day.
ISBN 978-0-8118-5609-6
[1. Collectors and collecting—Fiction. 2. Pets—Fiction. 3. Saint Patrick's Day—
Fiction.] I. Slonim, David, ill. II. Title.
PZ7.S3442Jc 2008
[E]—dc22
2007002050

Book design by Amelia May Anderson.
Typeset in Usherwood.
The illustrations in this book were rendered in pen and ink.

ISBN 978-0-8118-7949-1

Manufactured by C&C Offset, Longgang, Shenzhen, China, in August 2011.

1 3 5 7 9 10 8 6 4 2

This product conforms to CPSIA 2008.

Chronicle Books LLC
680 Second Street, San Francisco, California 94107

www.chroniclekids.com